BIG
N'T

This Little Tiger
ook belongs to:

_____

_____

_____

SNAKE CLUB! W

DO YC

LION PRIDE!

# CAN I JOIN YOUR CLUB?

John Kelly

Steph Laberis

LITTLE TIGER PRESS
London

Duck wanted to make some new friends.
So he decided to join a club.

"Hello," said Duck. "Can I join Lion Club?"

"Well," replied Lion. "I see you already have a
magnificent mane. But can you **ROAR** like a lion?"
He took a deep breath, puffed out his chest and . . .

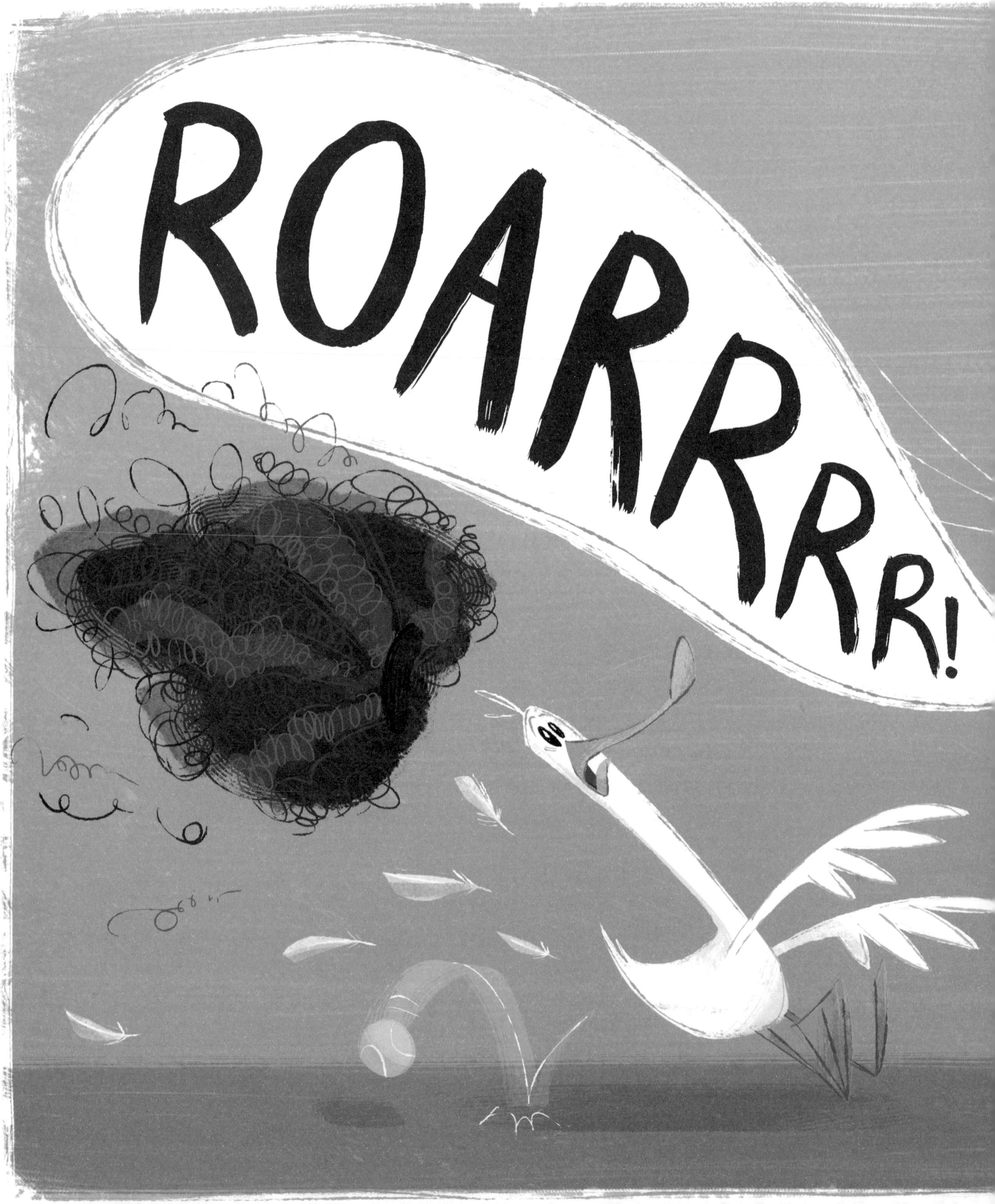
ROARRRRR!

Duck had a go. He took a deep breath, **puffed** out his chest feathers and . . .

"Application **DENIED!**" said Lion.

You're not really what we're looking for in Lion Club.

"Can I join Snake Club?" said Duck.
"Do you have any arms or legs?" said Snake.
"I've got legs and **WINGS!**"
smiled Duck proudly.

"That's a shame," yawned Snake.
"We don't really do arms, legs OR wings any more.
Can you at least **HISS** like a snake?"

Duck had a go. He narrowed his eyes, **stuck** out his tongue and . . .

"Can I join Club Elephant?" said Duck.

"How's your memory?"
asked Elephant.

Listen carefully and repeat after me.

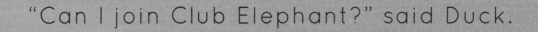

CLUB ELEPHANT

Diction

MATHLETE

"Your turn," said Elephant.

"I'm sorry," said Duck, "could you repeat that?
I was distracted by your trunk waving around."

"Well," huffed Elephant, "can you at least
**TRUMPET** like an elephant?"

He took a deep breath, flapped his
big ears and . . .

Duck had a go. He took a deep breath, **flapped** his tail feathers and . . .

"Application **DENIED!**" said Elephant.

CLUB ELEPHANT

MATHLETE

You're not really what we're looking for in Club Elephant.

Duck felt down but he knew what he had to do.

He started his **OWN CLUB!**

"Excuse me," said Tortoise. "Can I join Duck Club?"

"I'll have to ask you a question first," said Duck,
picking up his notepad and pen.
"Do you want to be in a club with me?"

"Yes, please," said Tortoise.

Duck put down his pen. "**APPLICATION . . .**"

Rabbit hopped up.
"Can I join your club?" she asked.

"Do you want to be in a club with us?" said Tortoise.

"Yes!" nodded Rabbit.

"Application **APPROVED!**" said Duck.

You are **exactly** what we're looking for in Our Club.

Soon **OUR CLUB** became quite popular.

OUR CLUB!

Cool! Quack!

THIS SIDE UP

And Duck let everyone in.
Because you can never have too
many friends.

To the original Duck.
Thanks for letting me join your club.
J K

For Rez, Fritzy and Nova. I am so proud to
have you all in my club.
S L

**LITTLE TIGER PRESS**
1 The Coda Centre, 189 Munster Road, London SW6 6AW
www.littletiger.co.uk

First published in Great Britain 2017
This edition published 2017

Text copyright © John Kelly 2017
Illustrations copyright © Steph Laberis 2017
John Kelly and Steph Laberis have asserted their rights to be identified as the
author and illustrator of this work under the Copyright, Designs and Patents Act, 1988

A CIP catalogue record for this book is available from the British Library

Printed in China • LTP/1400/1645/0916

2 4 6 8 10 9 7 5 3 1

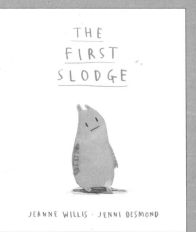
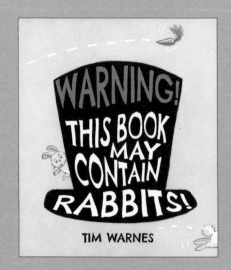
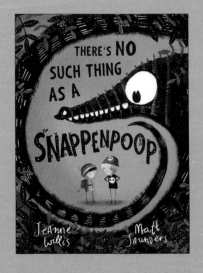

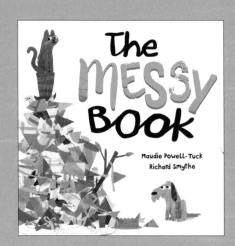
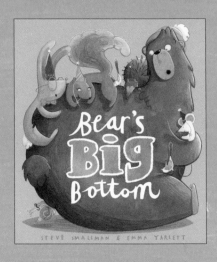